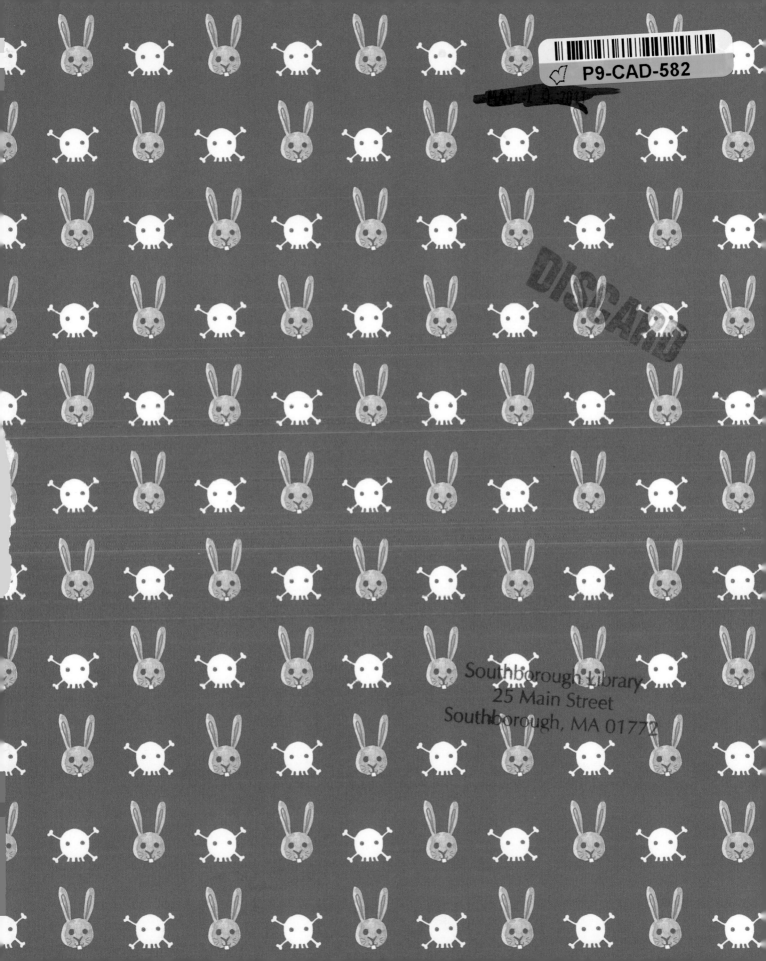

SMALL
SAUL

written and illustrated by

Ashley Spires

KIDS CAN PRESS

SMALL SAUL loved the sea.
He loved its vastness,
its calmness, its blueness.

He was meant to be on the water.
Even as a child, he dreamed
of a life at sea.

When he was old enough, Small Saul tried to become a sailor, but the Navy wouldn't have him.

YOU MUST BE **THIS TALL** TO JOIN THE NAVY

Fortunately, pirates aren't so picky, so he enrolled in Pirate College.

Small Saul was hardly a natural pirate. Being rough and tough just wasn't in his nature.

He was good at Intro to Swabbing the Deck, but he was easily distracted during Treasure Map Interpretation.

He did well in Navigation, but he lacked focus in Looting: The Basics.
He was born to sing sea shanties, not to hold a sword.

Despite these setbacks, he was determined to
graduate. Finally, after months of hard work,
Small Saul earned his Pirate Diploma.

Small Saul now had a chance
to travel the open seas.
He just needed to join
a pirate crew.

Even though Saul
was small, it looked like
no one had room for him …

... until a voice hollered from the only remaining ship at port: "Ahoy there! Climb aboard!" At last, Small Saul would be a real pirate!

But it didn't take long for the other pirates to notice
that something was different about Small Saul.

ARRRRRRRR

Even the captain began to wonder about his new crew member.

Small Saul knew that if he wanted to remain at sea, he would have to prove his worth as a pirate.

Pirate College had taught him that there are only three things pirates care about:

1.

Their ship

2.

Being tough

3.

Lots and lots of treasure

Small Saul needed to show that he cared about these things as well.

He began with the ship. Small Saul decided to add some
special touches to make *The Rusty Squid* a bit more homey.

Sadly, his efforts failed to
impress his crewmates.

Next, Small Saul
considered how to
be tough.

Since fighting wasn't for him,
he decided that a tattoo
would be perfect.

Unfortunately, the result didn't seem to intimidate anyone.

Redecorating the ship and demonstrating
his fierceness hadn't worked. His only
option was to get some treasure.
But he wasn't sure how ...

Small Saul thought about how to find treasure while he swabbed the deck.

He stewed about it through battles.

He mulled it over during kitchen duty.

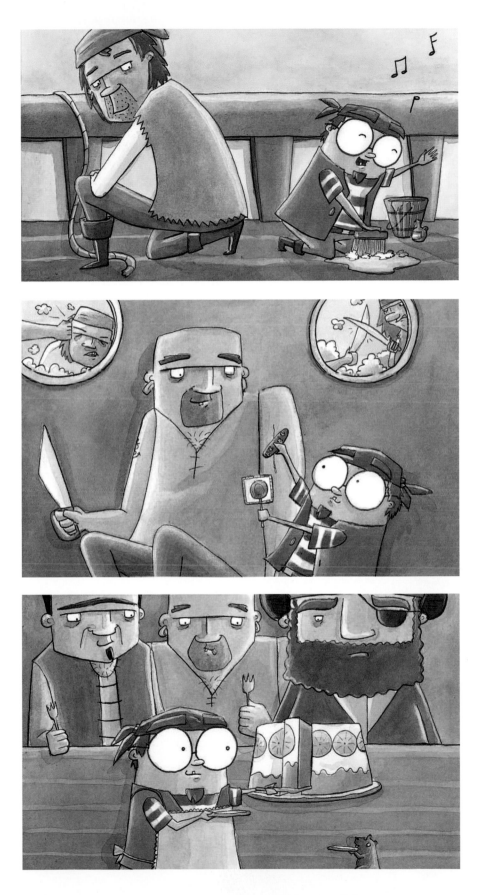

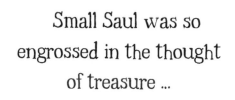

Small Saul was so engrossed in the thought of treasure ...

... that he didn't even notice when the captain pushed him overboard.

The Rusty Squid sailed away and left Small Saul behind.

Soon, mold began to build up on the ship's deck.

The crew was back to eating bland gruel and rat-nibbled bread.

And the cabins once again smelled of feet.

It was pirate life as usual, and the crew members of *The Rusty Squid* should have been happy about it. But they weren't. Even the captain couldn't adjust to the old pirate ways.

And that's when they realized:
Small Saul may not have been your
average pirate, but he had tried his
best. He had made their ship a home.
Just like treasure, Small Saul was rare.

The crew turned *The Rusty
Squid* around and rushed back
toward Small Saul, hoping
that it wasn't too late.

When the pirates apologized
for throwing him overboard,
Small Saul forgave them.

They were pirates, after all.
Throwing people overboard is
just something they do.

Small Saul was happy to be sailing
again and his shipmates were
happy to have him back.
He was where he was meant to be,
sailing the high seas and being a
pirate in his own special way.

For Dana, my one-of-a-kind friend

Text and illustrations © 2011 Ashley Spires

Kids Can Press acknowledges the financial support of the Government of Ontario,
through the Ontario Media Development Corporation's Ontario Book Initiative; the Ontario
Arts Council; the Canada Council for the Arts; and the Government of Canada,
through the BPIDP, for our publishing activity.

Published in Canada by
Kids Can Press Ltd.
25 Dockside Drive
Toronto, ON M5A 0B5

Published in the U.S. by
Kids Can Press Ltd.
2250 Military Road
Tonawanda, NY 14150

www.kidscanpress.com

The artwork in this book was rendered in ink, watercolor, water, flour,
a cup of sugar, a dash of vanilla and baked at 350.°
The text is set in McKracken.

Edited by Tara Walker
Designed by Karen Powers

This book is smyth sewn casebound.
Manufactured in Shen Zhen, Guang Dong, P.R China, in 3/2011 by Printplus Limited

CM 11 0 9 8 7 6 5 4 3 2

Library and Archives Canada Cataloguing in Publication

Spires, Ashley, 1978-
Small Saul / Ashley Spires.

ISBN 978-1-55453-503-3

I. Title.

PS8637.P57S63 2011   jC813'.6   C2010-904901-2

Kids Can Press is a l'ORUS™ Entertainment company

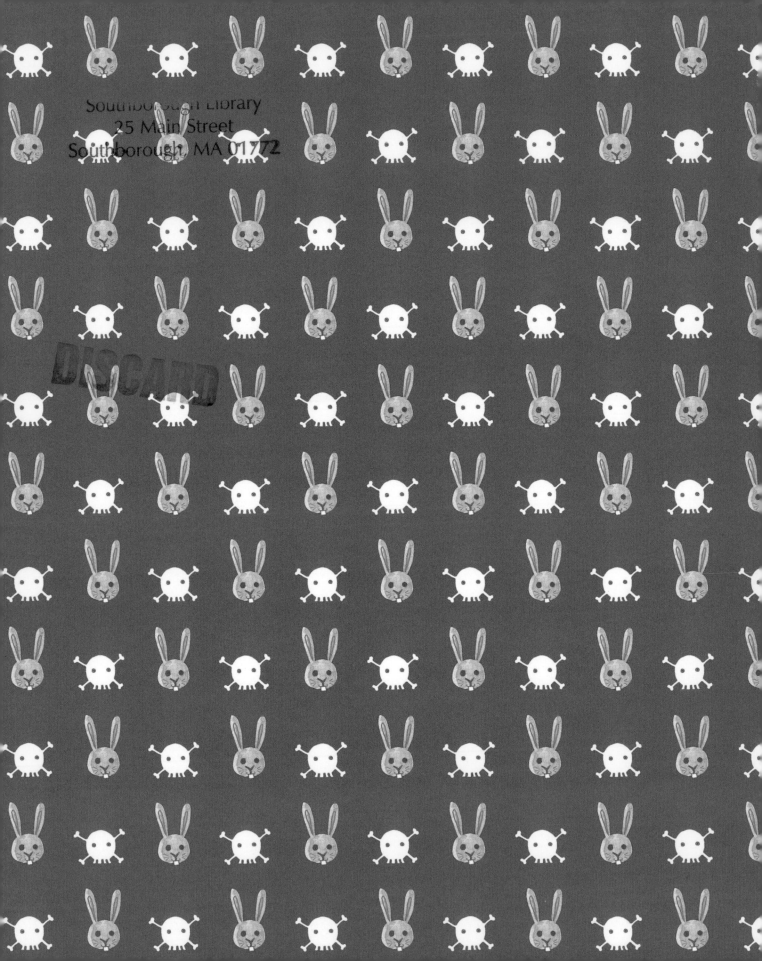